Science

JUST HELP!

How to Build a Better World

SONIA SOTOMAYOR

ILLUSTRATED BY
ANGELA DOMINGUEZ

PHILOMEL BOOKS

To Teresa Mlawer
*Thank you for building a community of readers for my books
and for so many others with your beautiful translations*

—S. S.

To my mom and family

—A. D.

A Letter to Readers

Ever since I was a young child, I remember my mother helping others. As a nurse, she went to work every day in a hospital and cared for people who were ill. She was also a good neighbor, helping friends with their medications and driving others to the doctor. Day after day and person by person, she made her neighborhood, her city, and the wider world a better place. She lived a life of service.

As I got older, I knew that I did not want to be a nurse, or a doctor, as my brother would become. I wanted to find a different way to serve my neighbors and my country and be a part of civic life and improve my community. I found my way through the law. Laws are the rules we all agree to live by to have a just society where we can be free and safe. Laws can be used to help and protect people.

But you do not have to be a lawyer or a judge or a doctor or a nurse to serve your community and participate in civic life. You can be a farmer who grows the food we all need to eat, a hotel housekeeper who helps visitors enjoy their travels, a banker who lends money to neighborhood businesses, a librarian who shares books, a firefighter who saves lives. You can run errands for people who cannot go out, volunteer at a food pantry, mentor a younger child who needs extra help, or register people to vote. Our communities need all of us to do our part, each of us like strings of yarn in a blanket, knitted tightly together by what we do.

Every day, you can make a difference by helping someone. Each time you do, you become part of something bigger than yourself. It may start small at first by helping younger siblings or cousins learn to tie their shoes, or bringing cookies to a new neighbor. Then it can grow from there when you start to see that the world is one very large neighborhood and that there is a lot we all need to do to make it healthy, safe, and clean for everyone. Building a better world is a big project, one that takes a lot of work, and is not always easy, but it begins with a simple question: How will you help today?

Sonia Sotomayor

ach day when Sonia woke up, her mother asked
her a question.
     "How will you help today?"
     Mami was a nurse who helped people at a hospital
every day. Sonia wanted to help too.
     So each morning, Sonia set about to have a good
answer for Mami's question.

One morning, Sonia knew just how she was going to help that day. She filled two shopping bags with candy bars, warm socks, nice soaps, sunglasses, pens, and notepads.

When Sonia boarded the school bus, the
driver helped her carry her bags up the steps.
"What's all this?" she asked Sonia.
"We're sending care packages to American
soldiers overseas," Sonia said.

When Sonia got on the bus, not one seat was free.
She did not know what to do. Then Booker and Skye
waved to her.

"You can sit with us," they said, squeezing
together to make room for Sonia.
"Thank you," Sonia said.

At school, Booker, Skye, and Sonia emptied their bags onto a table in the gym. Many kids had shown up to help.

For this service project, the kids sorted and packed the treats in boxes that postal workers would pick up later in the day.

Kiley was extra happy to help. Her mom was a soldier in the army, stationed far away. Kiley missed her every day, but it made her smile to think of her mom opening one of the care packages.

When she was done, Kiley gathered up plastic shopping bags and gave them to Brooklyn.

Brooklyn loved underwater animals. She was upset to learn that plastic bags humans dumped into the oceans made sea turtles sick. When she read about a worldwide campaign to save the sea turtles, Brooklyn joined in to help.

SAVE
THE
SEA TURTLES

She started a recycling program at school just for plastic bags.
After the service project in the gym, she had a lot more bags to add
to the new recycling bins.

After school, Gabriela and her brother Lucas
went to the playground. There was trash everywhere.
Gabriela thought about the recycling bins.

"Let's make today a park cleanup day," Gabriela
suggested to the other kids. They all agreed to help.

Afterward, Lucas took a piece of chalk and wrote
in big letters on the ground: KEEP OUR PARK CLEAN!
PLEASE DO NOT LITTER!

When Jasper got home, he saw that his room was a mess, just like the park had been. As he cleaned up, he found brand-new toys that he had never used.

Jasper decided to donate them to the children's hospital. Jasper remembered that when he was a patient there, he always felt better when the nurses brought him to the playroom. He wanted to help kids who were there now.

He brought the new toys next door to Maya, because
her dad worked as a janitor at the hospital, and he could
take the toys to the playroom.

Jasper's kindness reminded Maya that she had something special to give away too.

She picked out her favorite shirt from her clothes drawer. Maya loved it, but she knew someone who would love it more, especially today: her friend Simone.

Simone stood on the street corner with her
dad and her brother Miles. It was Election Day
and they were campaigning for their favorite
candidate for city council, who promised to build
more schools and playgrounds.

When Maya gave Simone the shirt, Simone was thrilled.

"It's just like a sparkly American flag! Thank you!" Simone said, and put it on over the shirt she was already wearing.

Simone and Miles were handing out flyers to everyone who passed by, including Samir and his mom.

"Mommy, it's Election Day! Did you vote yet?" Samir asked.

"No, I forgot!" his mom said.

"Well, let's go vote," Samir said. "My teacher said, 'Your vote is your voice in the community.'" Samir wanted his mom to use it!

The voting booths were set up in the senior center.
As Samir and his mom waited to vote, they saw Kunal
pushing John in a wheelchair. Kunal was there to help John
vote. John lived alone, and twice a week, Kunal spent the
afternoon at the senior center, visiting John and sharing snacks.

"Promise me when you're eighteen you will vote," John said as he stuck his I VOTED sticker on Kunal's shirt. "When I was young, I was part of a great struggle to get the right to vote. Now I never miss the chance."

"I promise!" Kunal said.

Later that evening, Sonia climbed into bed, and her mother asked her, "Sonia, how did you help today?"

Sonia thought about the service project for the soldiers, recycling the plastic bags, cleaning up the playground, and voting with Mami.

But she also remembered the bus driver who brought her to school safely, the postal workers who delivered the packages to the soldiers, the poll workers who guided voters, and her friends who helped in big ways and small.

"We all helped each other today," Sonia said.

As Sonia closed her eyes, she imagined that everything she did was like the yarn in the blanket her grandmother had made for her. It tied Sonia to everyone around her, even people she did not know, each one inspiring the next, knitting together a community that was safer, cleaner, wiser, healthier, and kinder.

Like Sonia, her friends, and her neighbors, when we all do our part, we all can have a good answer to Mami's question:

How will you help today?

Acknowledgments

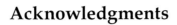

Each day I am inspired, and my energy is renewed, by the countless people who unselfishly improve our world in small and big ways. Your work keeps me from being discouraged about the world's problems. I keep hope alive because of you.

Ruby Shamir is an incredible collaborator, and I thank her for helping me to bring my book idea to life. I am grateful to Zara Houshmand for her wise counsel in all I write.

Angela Dominguez, you are such a gifted artist. I greatly appreciate your endless patience in responding to my vision for this book through your illustrations.

I am privileged to have an extraordinary editor, Jill Santopolo, and a superb team at Penguin Random House and Philomel Books. Thank you for your hard work and dedication.

My agents, Peter and Amy Bernstein, and my lawyers, John S. Siffert and Mark A. Merriman, provide me with wisdom and sound judgment that I treasure. I am deeply indebted to my assistants, Susan Anastasi, Anh Le, and Joanna X. Hernández, who are so important to me in accomplishing my work.

I have a long list of people who have provided insights into the various drafts of my book. Each one of you has improved my thinking, writing, and presentation. I thank you all for your many helpful suggestions. I list in alphabetical order: Theresa Bartenope, Talia Benamy, Jennifer Callahan, Louise Dubé, Eva Dundas, Cate Foster, Julia Foster, Lisa Foster, Robert A. Katzmann, Summer Ogata, Amy Richard, Carlos Santayana, Ricki Seidman, Gianna Semidei, Lisa Ledesma Wasielewski, and Rachel Wease.

PHILOMEL BOOKS

An imprint of Penguin Random House LLC, New York

First published in the United States of America by Philomel,
an imprint of Penguin Random House LLC, 2022

Visit us online at penguinrandomhouse.com.

Library of Congress Cataloging-in-Publication Data is available.

Printed in the United States of America.

ISBN 9780593206263

1 3 5 7 9 10 8 6 4 2

PC

Edited by Jill Santopolo

Design by Ellice Lee and Monique Sterling

Text set in Palatino

Artwork was rendered digitally using Procreate and Photoshop.